Where the River Begins

WHERE THE RIVER BEGINS

by Thomas Locker

Dial Books

E. P. Dutton, Inc.

NEW YORK

Published by Dial Books
A Division of E. P. Dutton, Inc.
2 Park Avenue | New York, New York 10016

Published simultaneously in Canada by Fitzhenry & Whiteside Limited, Toronto
Copyright © 1984 by Thomas Locker
All rights reserved
Designed by Jane Byers Bierhorst
Printed in Verona, Italy,
by Arnoldo Mondadori Editore
First Edition
COBE
10 9 8 7 6 5 4 3 2 1

Library of Congress Cataloging in Publication Data

Locker, Thomas, 1937 —
Where the River Begins.

Summary | Two young boys and their grandfather go on a camping trip
to find the source of the river that flows by their home.
[1. Camping — Fiction. 2. Rivers — Fiction. 3. Grandfathers — Fiction.] I. Title.
PZ7.L7945Wh   1984   [E]   84-1709
ISBN 0-8037-0089-X   ISBN 0-8037-0090-3 (lib. bdg.)

The art for each picture consists of an alkyd and oil painting,
which is color-separated and reproduced in full color.

To the memory of my teacher Joshua C. Taylor

Once there were two boys named Josh and Aaron who lived with their family in a big yellow house. Nearby was a river that flowed gently into the sea. On summer evenings the boys liked to sit on their porch watching the river and making up stories about it. Where, they wondered, did the river begin.

Their grandfather loved the river and had lived near it all his life. Perhaps he would know. One day Josh and Aaron asked their grandfather to take them on a camping trip to find the beginning of the river. When he agreed, they made plans and began to pack.

They started out early the next morning. For a time they walked along a familiar road past fields of golden wheat and sheep grazing in the sun. Nearby flowed the river – gentle, wide, and deep.

At last they reached the foothills of the mountains. The road had ended and now the river would be their only guide. It raced over rocks and boulders and had become so narrow that the boys and their grandfather could jump across.

In the late afternoon, while the sun was still hot, the river led them into a dark forest. They found a campsite and set up their tent. Then the boys went wading in the cold river water.

The first long day away from home was over. That night,
around the flickering campfire, their grandfather told Josh and
Aaron stories. Drifting off to sleep, they listened to
the forest noises and were soothed by the sound of the river.

Dawn seemed to come quickly and the sun glowed through a thick mist. The boys were eager to be off, but their grandfather was stiff from sleeping on the ground and was slower getting started.

The path they chose led them high above the river. On a grassy knoll they stopped to gaze around. The morning mist had risen and formed white clouds in the sky. In the distance the river meandered lazily. It was so narrow that it seemed almost to disappear. They all felt a great excitement, for they knew they were nearing the end of their journey.

Without a word the boys began to run. They followed the river for an hour or more until it trickled into a still pond, high in an upland meadow. In this small, peaceful place the river began. Finally their search was over.

As they started back, the sky suddenly darkened. Thunder crashed around them and lightning lit the sky. They pitched their tent and crawled inside just before the storm broke. Rain pounded on the roof of their small tent all night long, but they were warm and dry inside.

In the morning long before dawn they were awakened by a roaring, rushing sound. The river had swelled with the storm and was flooding its banks. They tried to take a shortcut across a field but were soon ankle deep in water. Grandfather explained that the river drew its waters from the rains high up in the mountains.

They came down out of the foothills in the soft light of late afternoon. The boys recognized the cliffs along the river and knew they were close to home. Their weariness lifted and they began to move more quickly down the road.

At last they reached their house on the hill. The boys raced
ahead to tell their mother and father about the place where the
river began. But their grandfather paused for a moment and
in the fading light he watched the river, which continued on as
it always had, flowing gently into the sea.